Russell Hoban
and
Quentin Blake

TROUBLE ON THUNDER MOUNTAIN

ff

faber and faber

First published in 1999
by Faber and Faber Limited
3 Queen Square London WC1N 3AU
Printed in Singapore.

A CIP record for this book
is available from the British Library

ISBN 0--571--19359--5

2 4 6 8 10 9 7 5 3 1

For Paulchen

Thunder
Mountain

The Family O'Saurus

to Endsville →

Mum O'Saurus and Dad O'Saurus and their
son Jim had lived on Thunder Mountain for
ages and ages and they were very happy there.
They grew parsnips and leeks and onions and
potatoes in their vegetable patch and they grew
rocks in their rock garden.

They had a TV and a video and they watched films like *Rocky Dinosaur - Secret Agent, Rocky Dinosaur on the Orient Express,* and *Rocky Dinosaur's Return Trip.* They also enjoyed *The Extinct Road Show* and *Mesozoic Challenge.*

One day the postman brought them a letter:

```
Dear Family O'Saurus,

  I am delighted to tell you that
Thunder Mountain has been bought by
Megafright International. We are
going to make it flat and build a
hi-tech plastic mountain theme park
on the flat place. This will be
called Megafright Mountain and it
will have robot monsters and a
Tunnel of Terror and other scary
rides. We are ready to start work
now so you have 24 hours (beginning
yesterday) to get out.

  Megafrightfully yours,

  J.M. Flatbrain, President
  Megafright International
```

"A hi-tech plastic mountain," said Dad. "It takes a man named Flatbrain to think of something like that," said Jim.

"Listen!" said Mum, "I hear heavy machinery coming up the road. I am worried about our vegetable patch."

"Maybe we could stomp on him and his machines and show him what flatness is all about," said Jim.

"Jim," said Dad, "any fool can resort to violence but that is not our way."

"What are we going to do then?" said Jim.

"I do not know," said Dad, "but I will think of something."

"Better do it soon," said Mum. "There go the parsnips."

"Good morning," said Mr Flatbrain. "Now it is time for you to leave because we are going to start blasting."

"We do not want to leave," said Dad. "This is our mountain and we want to stay here."

"This is not your mountain any more," said Mr Flatbrain. "Now it belongs to Megafright International."

"Thunder Mountain is so beautiful," said Mum. "How can you want to flatten it?"

"Thunder Mountain is just a lot of dirt and rocks with creepy-crawlies under the rocks and animals running around loose all over the place," said Mr Flatbrain. "Megafright Mountain will be clean and tidy with entertainment for the whole family and no ants when they picnic." He gave Dad a piece of paper. "There is a place for you down the road. Goodbye and good luck."

The O'Sauruses loaded their belongings on to their old pickup truck. They loaded their TV and video and their beds and sofas and tables and chairs. They loaded their curtains and carpets and pictures and bric-a-brac. They loaded their dishes and their pots and pans, their croquet set and cricket gear. They loaded their toolboxes and their buckets and wheelbarrows and shovels and pickaxes. They took a bag of seed potatoes with them too.

"Have you packed the Monsta-Gloo?" said
Mum to Dad.
"Yes," said Dad. "Everything is packed."

Off they went down the road. All the animals and birds from Thunder Mountain followed them. After a while they found some wasteground full of broken bottles, rusty bedsprings, broken bathtubs, and car seats with the stuffing coming out. Mum and Dad and Jim looked at their piece of paper. It said:

Dear Family O'Soupus,

This patch of wasteground has been reserved for you. We hope you will be pleased with this impravement.

Betterly yours,

A. Worser

"Worser could do better with his spelling," said Jim.

"That is the least of our worries," said Dad.

"This is a very ugly place," said Mum.

"It is very flat as well," said Jim.

"We will never sing here," said the birds.

"This ground smells bad," said the moles. "We do not want to dig here."

"This is not a very nice place but we are going to have to make the best of it," said Mum.

Just then they heard a big bang and they saw the top of Thunder Mountain go up into the air.

"You said you would think of something," said Jim to Dad.

"I am thinking," said Dad, "but nothing has come to me."

"I am thinking too," said Mum, "and I have an idea. But we shall need a little faith and a lot of Monsta-Gloo for it to work."

"We have plenty of both," said Dad.

"Tell us what to do," said Jim.

"First we need to see what they are doing with the bits of our mountain," said Mum.

When the robot monsters loaded the bits on to their trucks and drove away, the O'Sauruses and their friends followed them. They were careful to keep out of sight.

When the trucks came to a beautiful valley Mr Flatbrain said to his robot-monster foreman, "Dump everything here and we will fill in this valley and make it flat."

"OK, Boss," said the robot-monster foreman, and all the trucks dumped their loads in the valley.

When the Megafright trucks drove off, Mum said to everyone, "Do you know what I have in mind?"

"Yes," they said. They loaded all the bits of the top of Thunder Mountain into the pickup truck. When they got back they stuck them together with Monsta-Gloo.

When Mr Flatbrain and his crew came back to dump again they could not find what they had dumped before. "Amazing," said Mr Flatbrain. "Everything seems to have sunk right into the ground."

As soon as the Megafright trucks went back to the mountain the O'Sauruses and their friends came with the pickup truck and loaded up again. They had to build quite a large crane to lift up the top of the mountain so that they could slide the next part under it. They stuck it together with Monsta-Gloo.

"This is hard work," said Jim.

"Sometimes there is no easy way," said Dad, "but little by little we are getting it together."

"I think we should put up a curtain," said
Mum, "for privacy."

"Good idea," said Dad and Jim. Everybody
got busy with needle and thread and they made
a great big curtain. Then they made a frame to
hang it on.

The Megafright trucks made many more
trips and so did the O'Sauruses. Mr Flatbrain
did not notice the curtain until his plastic
mountain was almost finished. "What is
happening behind that curtain?" he said to his
robot-monster foreman. "What are those noises
I hear?"

"Bzzz, klonk," said the robot-monster
foreman. "Maybe big party?"

"Maybe you should lift a corner of the
curtain and have a look," said Mr Flatbrain.

22

"Zing zang, pfeh, pfft," said the robot-monster foreman.

"What are you trying to say?" said Mr Flatbrain.

"Got problem," said the robot-monster foreman. "No software for lift curtain."

Mr Flatbrain kicked the robot-monster foreman. "Try," he said.

"Pfeh," said the robot-monster foreman. It lifted one corner of the curtain and went inside. Dad was waiting for it with a screwdriver and a spanner.

"What can you see?" said Mr Flatbrain.

"Dark, Boss. Bzzz, burp. Very dark," said Dad in a robot-monster voice as he dressed up in the robot-monster parts as well as he could.

"Look again," said Mr Flatbrain.

"Big screen, Boss," said Dad. "Pictures moving. Heavy thriller." He made noises like the film *Rocky Dinosaur - Secret Agent*.

"That sounds like *Rocky Dinosaur - Secret Agent*," said Mr Flatbrain. "Are there a lot of people watching it?"

"Hundreds," said Dad.

"Good," said Mr Flatbrain. "That means there will be good crowds on Megafright Mountain. Now you should get back to work."

"OK, Boss," said Dad. He came out from behind the curtain in his robot-monster foreman disguise.

"You look bigger than you did before," said Mr Flatbrain.

"Feel great," said Dad.

"I am going back to the office now," said Mr Flatbrain. "Tomorrow is opening day and I want Megafright Mountain all finished and ready."

"Righty-o," said Dad. "Tomorrow all finish."

Behind the curtain the O'Sauruses and their friends had Thunder Mountain all put together. As soon as Mr Flatbrain left they put wheels under it and moved it next to Megafright Mountain. Among the O'Saurus friends were four hundred mole technicians and two or three thousand ants.

"There are the robots," said Dad to the ants. "You know what to do."

"Everything is go," said the ants. They crawled into the robots and changed their circuits.

"Bzzz, klonk, bzzt," said Dad. "This mountain – take apart."

"No prob," said Robot Monster Number One. The robot monsters took Megafright Mountain apart.

Then the O'Sauruses and their friends moved the real mountain back to where it used to be.

"Bzzt, burp," said Dad to the robot monsters. "Make tunnel."

The robot monsters made a tunnel in the real mountain.

"Zing, zang," said Dad. "Put in tracks for little train."

The robot monsters put in tracks all the way to Endsville many, many miles away.

"Put in little train," said Dad.

The robot monsters loaded all the bits of Megafright Mountain and the Tunnel of Terror on to the little train. Then they sent the train to Endsville.

The O'Saruses and their friends got ready
for opening day. They put up signs:

REAL
MOUNTAIN!

REAL DIRT
AND
ROCKS

BREATHE
REAL AIR!

They also put up another sign:

Mr Flatbrain arrived early on opening day.
"What is all this?" he roared. "It is all dirt and
rocks and creepy-crawlies again. What
happened to Megafright Mountain?"

"Bzzz, klonk," said Dad. "Please this way."
He led Mr Flatbrain to the tunnel entrance.
He put him on the little train and sent him off
to Endsville.

Then the O'Sauruses set up a stand on their mountain and they put up a sign:

Many people bought packed lunches and picnicked on the mountain. Some of them had never seen a mountain before. They met the animals.

They sang along with the birds. They interacted
with the ants. Everyone had a good time.

Others followed the signs to the tunnel, got
on the little train, and ended up in Endsville.
There they saw Mr Flatbrain trying to put the
plastic mountain and the Tunnel of Terror back
together again.

Everyone helped but it took a year and a half.

When it was finished, everyone said, "It looks like a plastic mountain."

When the Tunnel of Terror was in place everyone tried it out. Then some began to mutter. Others began to shout. "Megafright Mountain is not as good as a real mountain and the Tunnel of Terror is boring," they shouted.

Mr Flatbrain became megafrightened and he ran away to a town where nobody knew him.

He became a gardener and he made rock gardens in the shape of little mountains. Sometimes he made tunnels in them.